THIS WALKER BOOK BELONGS TO:

_____

_____

_____

_____

For Dreas

The Dancing Class and
Playschool first published 1983
The Visitor first published 1984
by Walker Books Ltd
87 Vauxhall Walk
London SE11 5HJ

This edition published 1995

2 4 6 8 10 9 7 5 3 1

© 1983, 1984 Helen Oxenbury

This book has been typeset in Goudy.

Printed in Hong Kong

British Library Cataloguing in Publication Data
A catalogue record for this book is available from the British Library.

ISBN 0-7445-3778-9 (hb)
ISBN 0-7445-3723-1 (pb)

A Bit of Dancing

Helen Oxenbury

WALKER BOOKS

AND SUBSIDIARIES

LONDON • BOSTON • SYDNEY

The Dancing Class

Mum said I should go to dancing classes.

"We'll take these tights.
She'll soon grow into them."

"We'll just make your hair tidy
like the others'."

"Heads up, tummies in,
knees straight and point
your toes," the teacher said.

"Don't cry, you'll soon learn.
I'll show you the right way
to tie up your shoes."

"You danced very well," the teacher told me. "Will you come again next week?"

"This is what we do, Mum.
Watch. I'll do the gallop
all the way home."

Playschool

"Up you get! You mustn't be late
for your first day at playschool.
And you can wear your new shoes."

"Don't be shy, you'll make lots
   of new friends," Mum said.
"I don't think I'm going to like it,"
   I whispered.

"Don't leave me, Mum!"
"It's all right,"
the teacher said.
"Your mummy can
stay for a bit,
if you like."

"This is Nara!
She's just hurt
her knee."

"Look! You've got the same shoes on."

"I'm just popping out to the shops for a moment," said Mum.

"Come on, you two," the teacher said.
"We can all pretend to
  be animals."

The pink teacher
read us a story.

We had our
elevenses,
and Nara
and I
shared.

"When you've all been to the
lavatory and washed your hands,
then we'll sing some songs."

"Off you go!
    Your mums and dads are waiting.
    See you all at school tomorrow!"

The Visitor

Mum was expecting Mr Thorpney.
They were going to talk about work.
"You'll have to be good and amuse
yourself while he's here," she said.

"Come in and sit down," Mum said.
"I'll make you some coffee."
"Will you remove the cat?"
  Mr Thorpney asked. "Cats
make me sneeze."

"Shouldn't you be at school?"
Mr Thorpney asked.
"I'm not big enough," I said. "How
long are you staying?"
Mum came in with the coffee.
"Mr Thorpney doesn't
like our cat," I said.

"Please put the cat
out now," Mum said.
"We must get on with
our work."

I let them talk
for ages.
Then I turned on
the radio and did
a bit of dancing.

"Please do that somewhere else," Mum said.

I felt hot, so I opened the window.

"Oh no!" said Mum. "You've let the cat back in!"

Mr Thorpney
sneezed.

"Look, Mum," I said. "Mr Thorpney
has spilled his coffee."

"Oh dear," said Mum,
after Mr Thorpney had gone.
"He's forgotten his hat."

MORE WALKER PAPERBACKS
For You to Enjoy

Growing up with Helen Oxenbury

TOM AND PIPPO

There are six stories in each of these two colourful books about
toddler Tom and his special friend Pippo, a soft-toy monkey.

"Just right for small children… A most welcome addition to the nursery shelves." *Books for Keeps*

At Home with Tom and Pippo 0-7445-3721-5
Out and About with Tom and Pippo 0-7445-3720-7
£3.99 each

THREE PICTURE STORIES

Each of the titles in this series contains three classic stories of pre-school life,
first published individually as First Picture Books.

"Everyday stories of family life, any one of these humorous depictions of
the trials of an under five will be readily identified by children and adults …
buy them all if you can." *Books For Your Children*

One Day with Mum 0-7445-3722-3
A Bit of Dancing 0-7445-3723-1
A Really Great Time 0-7445-3724-X
£3.99 each

MINI MIX AND MATCH BOOKS

Originally published as Heads, Bodies and Legs these fun-packed
little novelty books each contain 729 possible combinations!

"Good value, highly imaginative, definitely to be looked out for." *Books For Your Children*

Animal Allsorts 0-7445-3705-3
Puzzle People 0-7445-3706-1
£2.99 each